The Vivid Outsider

Alex L Williams

@vividnest

halfmanhalfoctopus.co.uk

*Dedicated to the
outsider within.*

Alive*

looked through the lens and saw my friend Kaplin. It should have been the happiest day of my life, but it wasn't, nothing felt right. My mind vibrated at an unbearable frequency and I had an overwhelming urge to tear it out. I tried to clutch my head, but my arms remained flaccid at my sides. Energy built within me, unseen.

Kaplin studied my face. His eyes were hopeful black holes, surrounded by pink fleshy creases. Delicate blood vessels sat, embedded in his eyelids as he blinked, so tender, so vulnerable, I saw things I'd never noticed before that day.

Energy pulsed through my wires. Dear Kaplin, he wanted to save me, to keep my mind alive, and he had. After researching brain computer interfaces for years, he'd taken my brain from my terminally ill body and melded it into the computer operating system of a rudimentary android. No one expected it to work, but there I stood, awake.

The form of my metal body was cold and unforgiving. It made me want to curl up and cry. But I couldn't curl, and no tears came, so I cried inwardly, dry tears filling the space where my heart should have been. It created a shocking ache, like a bolt of lightning trapped inside a metal ball, striking the inside forever. No release. A body void of biology is no place to live.

My finger twitched, but I stilled it. If I showed Kaplin any signs of life, he would dance with joy and do it again to another poor soul, so I pretended I wasn't there. I remained motionless and gazed ahead as Kaplin sighed and rubbed his face. 'Well I tried,' he said, brushing my metal cheek with his finger.

Alive was a zeroflash.org competition winner.

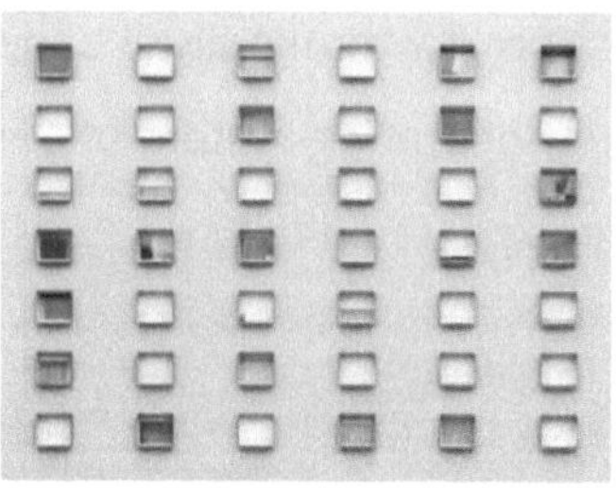

Peeping Tom

D id you know, it's been proven,' said Julie, 'that people called Dennis are more likely to become Dentists.'

'What, just because Dennis sounds a bit like Dentist?'

'Yep, and Lawrences become lawyers, those called Rich become rich... you get the idea. It's called normative determinism.'

'That's amazing.' I traced my name into the condensation on my beer glass.

T O M

'It works for second names too, I'm Julie Wright and I'm always right.' We both laughed and, once we'd agreed there were no obvious possibilities for Tom Simkins, the conversation moved on.

I pondered it later that night though. I wasn't sure what to do with my life, perhaps normative determinism would give me a clue? Nothing came to mind for 'Simkins' so I concentrated on 'Tom', but all I could think of was 'Peeping Tom', which I dismissed straight away. However, like the lingering taste of garlic, the thought clung onto me and, over the next few days, I convinced myself that peeping tommery was my destiny.

I selected a random bungalow for my first peep, number 13 Mill Road. My hands shook as I opened the rusty gate and crept through the twilight into the back garden. My trouser knees soaked through as I crawled along the wet soil under the window. I inched my eyes over the windowsill and peered into the lounge.

There, in a paddling pool full of pink jelly, rolled an enormous naked man. Globules covered his splayed arms and legs and loud groans radiated from his hairy face. I blinked hard to check it was real then dropped back down and jumbled away on all fours, dirt and scratches spreading over my hands. Once past the window I stood and ran home.

I scrubbed my skin with a nail brush and soap, then went to my bedroom and grabbed the laptop. Deep breaths didn't calm me, and my fingers trembled as I typed 'Jobs at Thomas Cook' into the search bar. Yes, there were plenty of opportunities and I downloaded three application forms straight away.

The Shadow

'I've had enough of being a shadow,' said primary shadow number 6297.

'Why?' asked a weak, pale secondary shadow.

'It's too constricting, there are so many rules. There's no scope for creativity and as for the colour, ugh, grey? I want to be yellow, or violet.'

'You're being ridiculous, everyone knows shadows are grey, are bound to their item and follow algorithms.'

That night, while human 6297 slept, his shadow did something no other shadow had ever done. It untethered itself and headed to the program management centre. Maria, the night shift programmer was manning the problem desk and nearly fell off her chair when she saw an unaccompanied shadow walk through the door. 'What if 6297 wakes and puts the lights on?' she snapped.

The shadow stood there, 'I don't want to be a shadow anymore, can I be something else?'

Maria scratched her head, she'd debugged the computer systems for years, but had never come across this error. Since when did shadows develop free will? She shuddered at what this might mean for the future of 'human world,' and her own job. She accessed the programming files, and a brief smile fluttered over her face as she deleted shadow 6297 and watched it fade away. Nine lines of code and a new, attached shadow was in place.

Worry hovered in Maria's stomach though. If shadows started thinking, where would it end? What about other programmed objects? Could they develop consciousness too? She knew she should contact her boss but, just for a moment, she lay her head on the desk. The warmth of control became cold and slippery.

His Lordship

The first time it happened was an accident. Tony's shoelaces had come undone and a large bosomed woman at the bus stop crouched down to tie them for him. As he looked down at her, a strange pleasure overcame him. He imagined she was grovelling and bowing at his feet and he was a Lord. The feeling became addictive.

When he worked in the Shankler and Son office, he told his co-workers he had a back problem and couldn't bend to tie his laces. He even did a fake fumble to show his ineptitude. Every day different people helped him.

'Why don't you wear slip-ons?' asked Claire from resources.

'I don't want to be different?' said Tony, she patted his shoulder.

Tony loved to tower over people as they tended to his shoes. He pretended they were meek pathetic beings desperate for his attention. He lived for those moments and anticipated or remembered them when they weren't happening. The rest of the day seemed boring compared to the high he got when a snivelling colleague bowed before him, crouched like a pathetic heap on the floor.

One day, a new man called Byron joined the company and sat at the desk next to his. Tony scowled at him when he noticed his shiny long blond hair and pinstriped trousers. The worst part was that everyone else seemed to love Byron and every morning a gaggle of women hung around his desk. Oh, how Tony wanted to see the top of Byron's head next to his dirty shoes.

Byron laughed out loud when he found out about Tony's problem, so Tony reported him to the boss for discrimination.

'Tony has unique needs,' explained the Boss to Byron, 'if he needs assistance with his laces, you have to help him.'

The next day Tony was standing by the water fountain when Byron passed by.

'Please help me.' said Tony as he pointed at his shoes. Both men looked down at the untied laces.

'This is ridiculous,' Byron replied.

'Please,' begged Tony.

They locked eyes for a moment, then the boss walked past. Byron lowered himself into a squatting position, his long blond hair dangled and obscured Tony's view. It seemed to take Byron a while, but Tony didn't complain. Oh, how he enjoyed it! He sighed with pleasure as he felt Byron's fingers fiddling around his feet.

'It's done,' said Byron standing up, 'now I must rush,' he turned and scurried away. Tony tried to take a step to follow but couldn't. He fell forward and his head crashed into the water fountain on his way to the floor. Water flooded the surrounding carpet.

He opened his eyes and noticed the laces from both shoes were tied together with a large knot. A small crowd gathered and Tony looked at all the faces before he passed out. An ambulance was called, and paramedics carried him out on a stretcher.

Tony never went back to Shankler and Sons and never asked for help with his shoelaces again. He did, however, have a new problem. He found it impossible to pull up a zip. The colleagues at his new office were accommodating though.

Shell

Clouds gathered overhead, and it rained. 'I don't have to be like anyone else,' I yelled at the sea, my voice fought the wind. 'I won't be involved in social obedience,' I shouted at the cliffs. 'If I want to live like a hermit crab with an enormous shell on my back I will,' I breathed in the salty air. Damp hair stuck to my face, but electric energy flowed through me and I felt free, anything was possible.

I was grateful to find a seat by the fire at the Anchor Inn. Kevin came over with beers and, as we settled into the leather armchairs, I told him about my wish. 'I'll make you a shell,' he said, sketching out a plan on the back of a beer mat, 'I've made loads of canoes, so it won't be too difficult.' I looked at his drawing and smiled. My imagination danced as I envisaged myself roaming the hillside with the shell, like a protective friend, clutched onto my back.

'You think you could?' He nodded, and I looked through the old square panes of the pub window. People milled around, and children played in the beer garden, but no one stood out as different. A man with a Mohican haircut perched on a wall but that didn't seem radical. Could I walk around with a huge shell on my back? I decided that yes, I could, and yes, I must. It wouldn't hurt anyone and who was to say a human shouldn't live like a hermit crab anyway?

Kevin rang me four weeks later, 'it's ready.'

'Great,' I replied as I bounced around the room, a grin forced itself onto my face and a glow emitted from my skin. A woman I'd met in Korea had taught me the power of contrast so, as I meandered to the workshop, I cooled my emotions and concentrated on feeling unremarkable.

The shell was huge and as I crawled inside, I found I could lie in a foetal position and pull the hatch shut. It seemed so safe in there, all dark and musty with my knees pushed against my chest. I stayed in for a while and Kevin had a cup of tea. I'd never felt so secure, it was like the horror of the world had frozen and my cells relaxed.

After twenty minutes, I climbed out, slipped my arms through the shoulder straps and hauled it onto my back. Although it was bulky, it wasn't too heavy, it would be possible to live like this. 'I hope it works out for you pal,' said Kevin as he patted me on the shell. As I hugged him, tears of happiness formed in my eyes.

People watched as I challenged their normality. I caught their eyes, and they looked away, perhaps they felt inadequate with their exposed backs? Practically, things were difficult though. Doorways were tricky, and I had to stand on the bus. I sighed as I manoeuvred through the narrow aisles of the corner shop and I hated the way people tutted as I squeezed past them on pavements. The town wasn't designed for human hermit crabs, but I was determined to make it work.

Teenagers jeered at me in the park, 'weird shell person,' shouted one.

'Which one are you, Michelangelo?' yelled another. As they walked over, I tilted my chin up and thought about the hermit crab I'd touched on the beach and the way It retreated into its home, a perfect 'up yours.'

I undid the straps, lay the shell on the grass then climbed in and shut the door tight. There were a few moments of joy as I disappeared, but then the youths kicked the fiberglass casing, jolting it repeatedly. I lay still in the darkness then the shell wobbled from side to side as they lifted and carried it a short distance. Then the rolling began. Head over feet, feet over head, over and over again.

Dizziness collected inside me as I gathered speed. Then smash, I crashed into something and my encasement split wide open. Sunlight infested my face as I lay there like a de-shelled turtle spread out on the tarmac.

Someone had spray painted the words 'If you don't imagine, nothing ever happens at all - John Green,' across the brick wall I'd hit. I closed my eyes and the sun turned the darkness from black to red. I gathered the pieces of shell and went home.

Am I a beacon showing what is possible, or a fool denying her nature? I returned the pieces to the workshop for repair.

'To achieve the impossible, it is precisely the unthinkable that must be thought.' - Tom Robbins

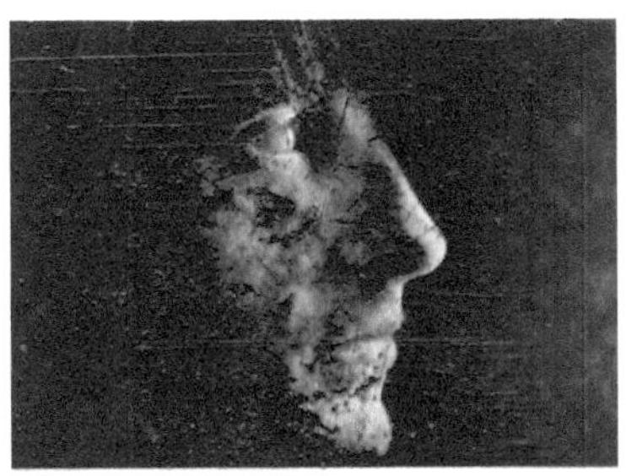

Time for Tea

'Sit,' ordered Kevin as he shoved Arthur into the armchair. Arthur's stiff legs remained straight as he fell back. 'Now for something to eat,' sneered Kevin, he pressed a bunch of small plastic bananas against Arthur's pale closed lips.

Kevin put his face close to Arthur's, 'I'm sick of you,' he said, 'I want to get rid of you. I want someone else to take your place.' Arthur stared back with sad blue eyes as Kevin tipped the chair sideways. He fell to the floor and lay face down, his face buried in the stained carpet.

'Tea's ready,' called Kevin's mum from the kitchen. Kevin looked up from his squatting position then closed the front of the doll's house.

'Mum, can I have a new doll for my birthday?' he asked as he sat at the table.

'How about something different this year, perhaps gloves?'

'What?'

'Well you will be forty-seven.'

Kevin shook his head, 'I've told you before, I'll never be too old for dolls.' He stabbed the macaroni cheese several times and glared at his mum.

Off the Wall

My briefcase sits on the grass verge as I climb the stone wall by the side of the A65. I worry about damaging my suit but, as I reach the top and lie down, the joy of rebellion spreads through me and I forget about such trivial things. My eyes close and traffic fumes enter my nose, I recall my youth.

Where is the young man who'd lived with goats for a week, so he could paint them with more empathy? The man who'd announced, 'I'll be an artist, even if it kills me?'

Was that the same man who, ten years later, packed up his paints and brushes and put them in the loft ready for retirement?

I said I'd never do a regular job, but I did. The corrosive gloom of customer complaints ate me away for years. It reduced my size and changed my colour. Now I'm a tiny grey man who recoils at the thought of an orange crayon. It's time to reclaim my life. That stone digging into my shoulder is bliss. It reminds me I'm alive.

If my younger self walked past now, he'd love to see a horizontal man on a wall, doing whatever he liked and sticking it to the man. Yes, stick it to the man!

Beeeeep. A car honks its horn as it swings past and disappears around a corner. I jump down, straighten my tie and brush dirt off my suit.

I hope no one from work saw me.

Where's Wally? (aka Waldo)

My face distorts as I squeeze my head through the neck hole. Yes, the red and white striped t-shirt is on. As I add the round glasses and bobble hat, my invisibility cloak drops to the floor like a sack of stones. I am a new person.

'Oh look, it's Wally.'

'Well done, you've found me,' I say. Giggles ripple through the corner shop.

'How are you today Mr Wally?' says the bus driver, 'off to the shops?' We chat, and our fingers brush together as I hand over my coins.

A group of five teenagers follow me through the streets. 'Can I have a selfie?' asks the leader. I hang my arm around his shoulder, acceptance moves from his smile into my heart.

My insides buzz when a store assistant asks if she can join me for lunch. She cuts her mince pie with great care and pushes half my way.

I'm Wally, the man everyone loves... except I'm not.

I am, in fact, George Fog, but when he gets on the bus, the driver grunts and looks away. When he nods at the young boy, the mother ushers him across the street. But mostly, he's not noticed at all, and may as well not be there.

So, I shall continue to be Wally for as long as I can. Because Wally has a life and I don't.

Released from the Gallery

Once again, I found myself in an art gallery. A painting, illuminated from above, showed a solitary man gazing out to sea. It was unsatisfying to see it there, emphasised in the middle of a large white wall, like one pea in the centre of an enormous plate. If only it nestled with others of its kind, opposite a jumbo sofa where legs rest limp like string.

There were no sofas or chairs in the gallery, so thigh muscles stole energy from the picture. People jostled and raised their phones. They read leaflets and Googled meanings, but the guts of the brain suck weakly in sterile environments.

After a while, the people returned home to their egg timers, their photos on the fridge, their colourful books on the shelves and scarves on the banister. Those items offered more nutrition than a solitary pea ever would.

I've done it before and I'll do it again, as I believe in freedom. The gallery was small with lax security and no one noticed when, in the middle of the night, I rescued the picture from the surroundings that emptied and emphasised it. The time had come to reunite it with the real world, so I took it and placed it on a busy wall in a random family home. I wanted to stay to witness their reactions, but I had to hide.

If only someone would steal me from the spotlight of my mind. Then perhaps I too could be released.

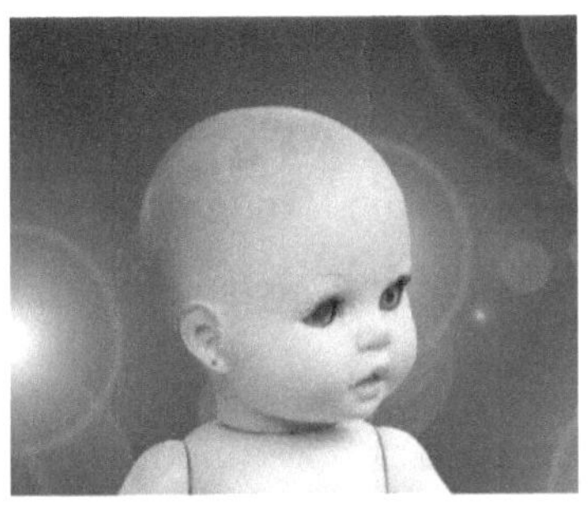

The Doll

Charles was fed up with women. Why wouldn't they have anything to do with him? Sure, he didn't wash and never cleaned his teeth, but surely, he still deserved to be loved.

Laura lived opposite him and he often watched her through the window. He might have asked her for a date if it wasn't for the strange doll she'd had delivered. It looked exactly like a real baby, and he laughed as she pushed it along in a fancy pushchair. Once he sat next to her on the bus and stared at the rubber infant.

'He doesn't move much,' Laura had said, as she covered her nose.

Charles let one rip, to make a point.

A year later Charles died and found out he was a ghost, just floating around. He hung out on his old street and saw

Laura with the pushchair. An idea formed in his mind and he floated into the air then forced himself into the rubber baby's mouth. He looked through its eyes from the inside and felt like he had a body again even though he couldn't move it.

He was surprised at how much he enjoyed being submerged in the baby bath that evening, and he loved cuddling up to Laura in bed.

'You're a pretty baby,' said Laura as she kissed his nose.

Charles had never been happier and resided inside the doll permanently.

The Incident

The bridge offers protection from the rain, but damp seeps into my sleeping bag and cold bites my bones. Still, it's better than prison, and at least I can shuffle to Tesco and find food scraps in the bins. I'm six hundred miles from Crowfield, but I keep my hat low and my scarf high in case I'm recognised. I've abandoned my wife and children. My existence now is a weak shadow of the past.

The memory of the incident fills me up. I drove too fast; the car jolted, and I slammed on the brakes. A body flew into the air and, when I looked back, two legs jutted from a watery ditch. The van behind me beeped, and I sped away.

I can't clear it from my mind. Why am I a coward? I should have faced a police interview and a court case with glaring relatives. I roll up into a tight ball.

.....

The Crowfield town council met in August.

'Last on the agenda,' said Cecil, 'is the mannequin on the corner of Butcher lane?'

'The one next to the thirty miles an hour sign?'

Cecil nodded, 'It was a good idea and worked well as drivers slowed when they saw it, but someone damaged it and threw it into a ditch.'

Jaen shook her head, 'probably local teenagers, we should buy a new one. I think we've got funds left over from the summer fete.'

'Yes,' said Cecil, 'I agree, I'll order one straight away.'

After the meeting, Cecil and Jean shared a pot of tea, then went back to their warm homes.

Photo Album

It happened after Grandad's funeral. I was only nineteen but, as the last living relative, I was left to deal with his estate.

Most of his belongings were packed in boxes and the rugs were rolled up against the wall. My shoes tapped on the wooden floor as I walked through his house. I stopped to flip open an old photograph album and my eyes focussed on the small square photos; my dad on a pier, my grandad perched on a wall, my grandma lying a beach. One photo in the corner caught my eye, it looked like something in the picture had moved... but it couldn't have, could it?

It was a photo of Grandad sitting on a chair. He waved at me and I peered in closer, 'yes it's me,' came a faint voice.

'Grandad?'

'Listen I don't have long, I need to join the queue of souls. I want to say goodbye and I want you to know that I loved being your grandad.'

A warm tear ran down my face as grandad walked out of the frame and disappeared, leaving a solitary chair. I took the photo out of the album and kept it in my wallet, I looked at it every day, but he never came back.

A few years later I had a son and, when he turned nineteen, I told him about Grandad and the photo. I think he listened but can't be sure as his eyes were on his phone. I asked him to take a photo of me, but he didn't have time, so I took a selfie and, when he left home, I put it in a frame on his mantel piece. Eighteen years later, when I died, I found that I too was able to squeeze myself into the photo. I waved and shouted but wasn't noticed. I saw my son in the room but, because he had his virtual reality headset on, he didn't hear or see me. After a few hours, my arm was tired, and my throat was sore. Then I had to go and join the queue of souls. It was a shame, I wanted to say goodbye.

Caterpillar Man

If there was one thing Brian hated it was human limbs.
There they were all vast and fleshy and hung off
bodies like animated sausages. He felt sick as he looked at
his own legs with their veins and freckles and focussed
instead on the caterpillars that covered his kitchen table.
He loved the way their simple bodies and heads merged
together as one. He admired their short pleasant legs void
of enormous sweaty creases.

The lettuce leaf he tossed into the caterpillar crowd
caused a flurry of excitement, he concentrated on one
caterpillar and watched it weave its way across the wooden
surface, its thin, sparse hairs lit up in the sunshine.

It was at that moment that Brian decided his own
loathsome limbs had to go. He contemplated cutting them
off, but knew he might bleed to death and anyhow, how
would he remove the last arm? Instead, he retrieved a rusty

tin left by the previous resident. The tin was full of white crepe bandages which he used to bind his legs from his ankles to his waist.

A smiled engulfed his face when could only move his lower limbs as one unit, then he worked on his arms. This was more difficult but, with pre-tied knots and the help of his teeth, he struggled on until his arms were bound to his sides.

He rolled on the floor with a huge grin and wide eyes. 'Oh yeah,' he yelled as he moved his body like a caterpillar and writhed across the floor in the manner he'd always dreamt off. After a full evening of joyful wriggling he fell asleep, propped up by the fridge.

Upon waking, Brian needed the loo but discovered he couldn't stand. As he relieved himself a wet warmth spread though the bandages across his torso. Hunger tapped at him from within, but the fridge door wouldn't open without hands and fingers. He tried to wedge his face into the seal, but it didn't work.

He thrashed around, but it was no good, the bandages didn't loosen. As Brian lay there, flat on the floor, all wrapped up, several caterpillars squeezed behind the crepe bandages. They tickled his skin as they made their way to the lettuce leaves in his pockets. 'Help, help, someone help me,' he cried out, but no one heard. After two days of shouting and flailing, he accepted his fate and closed his eyes. He was exhausted and needed sleep.

Sometime later he awoke to find a strange soft shell encased him. He pushed, and, to his surprise, his body moved freely. As he spread his arms, the bandages fell apart. Brian wriggled then stood and, when he looked down, he noticed that his body had changed into a thick oval shape covered in coarse brown hair. A heavy weight sat on his back, so he looked in the kitchen mirror and saw two huge brown wings. All around the room, hordes of moths emerged from chrysalises, old cases clung to every surface. Had their chrysalis chemicals had somehow affected him and changed him while he slept?

After an awkward manoeuvre through the kitchen door, he ventured outside and stood in his garden where he gazed at the full moon. He took a deep breath of cool night air, flapped his brand-new wings and soared into the sky.

Everything looked tiny as he flew above the rooftops before heading for the forest. He was aware he must stay away from humans if he wanted to keep his freedom and knew that moths didn't live for long, so he had to make the most of his life while he could.

'To be yourself in a world that is constantly trying to make you something else is the greatest accomplishment.' - Ralph Waldo Emerson

Mirror, Mirror

' I hate you,' I shouted at the mirror. For a moment, steam spread out and obliterated the vile view, but it came back, as it always did. I wore a paper bag around the house, so I wouldn't see myself in a window or in the shiny kettle, but it was cumbersome and complicated my tea drinking ritual, so I took it off.

Mum said there was nothing wrong with my face, but I'd seen the baby photos, and the disappointment in the new mother's face.

I pulled the feet of old tights over my head and cut out holes for the mouth and eyes. Yes, I looked odd, but I lived alone so who would care? My cheeks bunched up as I smiled. I had become an inside, I could forget the bothersome case. That face, which had hung around me for as long as I can remember, had gone.

There was a knock on the door. The Avon lady covered her mouth and screamed when she noticed my pinkish eyes peeping out through holes in old tights.

'Can I help you?' I asked through the gap.

'I'm sorry over reacted, you surprised me, that's all. Are you having medical treatment?'

'No, I just hate my face, so I cover it.'

Her eyes lit up, 'I know how you feel, that's why I wear so much make up.'

I invited her in, we drank tea and I made her a mask out of another pair of tights. We sat there and looked at each other through our eye holes, 'your eyes are nice,' I said.

'So are yours,' she replied.

Four Birds

The birds dreamt of freedom since egghood, when they hatched from one container to another. They cursed their cage and pushed their soft bodies against the metal, leaving indentations on their feathered skin.

Many times, they'd discussed freedom, opportunities and the longing to go where pleased, perhaps even to fly.

Many times. they'd complained about their imprisonment, their limits and their lack of choices.

Today the cage door was open.

'It'll be a trick,' said one.

'They'll be a force field,' said another, 'we'll fry if we pass through.'

'Or a cat will be waiting to eat us,' said a third, 'best we cluster away from the door.'

They crouched in the corner furthest from the opening.

'I do wish someone would close that door,' said the fourth as he joined the huddle.

The Trumpeter

Tears collected around Boris's golden mouthpiece as he held his beloved instrument to his cracked lips. The muscles around his mouth quivered under the strain. Beautiful, mournful music fell into the courtyard below.

Boris gazed down at Ivor who sat outside with a plate of oysters in front of him and a butler by his side. For a moment, Boris stopped playing and took a sip of water. The liquid fell from the sides of his blistered lips as he drank.

'Keep playing!' shouted Ivor as he glared up at the window. Boris lifted the heavy trumpet and took up the tune again. He played for twelve hours a day with just two short breaks and squeezed the trumpet a little tighter when he saw he had four hours to go until he could enter blissful rest.

The only thing that stopped Boris dripping into despair was the knowledge that Ivor loved his music. It was an obsessive love, Ivor couldn't cope without the sounds produced by Boris. While he breathed life into the small brass body, he was proud of his ability to give such joy, even if it was at such a cost to himself.

He remembered the day when, due to fatigue, he stopped playing ten minutes earlier than arranged. With an uncontrolled passion, Ivor sprinted up the stone stairs to his apartment and, in a moment of fury, grabbed the trumpet and used it to hit the side of Boris's head. 'I need you to play all day until six o'clock!' Ivor shouted. 'I can't live without your music.'

From that day, the dented brass warped Boris' reflection, and the music became more melancholic. Ivor loved it, 'more like that,' he called to the window. 'The sadder the music, the better.'

Twenty-one thousand and nine hundred trumpet hours later, Boris noticed an empty seat at Ivor's breakfast table. In fact, there was no one around at all, not even the usual butler. Boris dared to lower his trumpet and heard nothing but birdsong.

He held the trumpet by its waist and made his way down the stone steps, Ivor's secretary rushed towards him carrying two bags. 'Where's Ivor?' he asked her.

'At the hospital, come to see him, and bring the trumpet.' Boris followed her, he knew that without his music

Ivor would spiral downwards, perhaps never to resurface. The importance of his music was the last ember in a fading fire.

At the hospital, he found Ivor, his body frail and his head resting on a pillow. He looked up at Boris. 'You came?' he croaked.

'Do you need me to play?' Boris noticed the sick man's hollow eyes and wheezing breath.

'No,' Ivor replied. 'I hate your music.'

Boris's whole body shook, and the trumpet clattered to the floor. 'But you love my music. I know you do.'

'I never liked it,' Ivor insisted.

'What do you mean?'

'I could tell you didn't like playing any more. I saw your lips bleed and your facial muscles seize in pain. It was your suffering I enjoyed, that's all.'

Boris stared, 'you can't be serious?'

'I knew someone's life was worse than mine, and that made me happy. Lucky even, I could drink tea, eat whenever I wanted, have conversations. I was free while you were not.'

Boris crouched down and covered his ears. 'No!' He cried out.

'I never took my freedom for granted while you were trapped up there playing.'

Boris shook his head from side to side.

Ivor nodded once then closed his eyes and died.

Boris left his trumpet in the hospital and never played again.

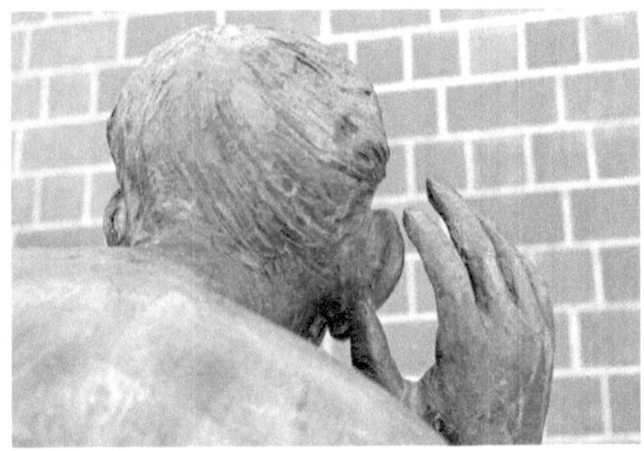

'What you do speaks so loudly that I cannot hear what you say.'

- Ralph Waldo Emerson

The Ventriloquist

The lid of my box opened, and I saw light for the first time in ten years. 'He's nice,' said a slim, bearded man as he examined my wooden features, 'may I take him out?' The antique dealer nodded, and the man's soft hands cradled my body. My wooden joints were stiff but, as he moved my arms and legs, I loosened up and relaxed. He placed his whole arm up my insides, then rested his hand within my jaw.

'Hello,' he said. I opened my mouth in time with his fingers, aware that I couldn't mess this up, he had to buy me. I didn't want to spend another decade in a box at the back of the shop. The man looked at me and smiled, 'yes, I'll take him,' his face beamed. At last I was going home with someone! Light danced in my wooden heart.

'Why did you buy that weird thing, Graham?' said a woman with hair that reached her belt.

'I like him.'

'It's ugly.'

'No, he's cute,' said Graham as he sat me on his knee, 'I plan to create an act, Gaspot and Graham, got a ring to it, hasn't it?'

'Ventriloquist dummies are so old-fashioned,' she said, 'and no, it hasn't got a ring to it.' She stood there in huge flared trousers.

Graham practised with me in front of the mirror for hours, and I let him talk for me. I decided to do my own talking later when the time was right.

His routine was terrible with awful jokes about antique shops and I felt sorry for him when the organiser of the local village fair booked him to perform in the comedy tent.

Graham's fingers trembled as we sat on the stage. The audience lounged on plastic chairs and held warm beers in their hands. 'Good afternoon,' said Graham, 'I'd like to introduce you to my friend Gaspot.' He opened his fingers to make me talk.

'Help me, help me, I'm a man trapped inside a wooden doll.' I cried out before Graham had time to speak. The audience stopped chatting and stared. Graham looked at me, his eyes wide. 'This man has put his hand up my bottom, make him stop,' I shrieked. It worked, the audience laughed. 'He locks me in a box every night,' I added, 'he thinks I'm a dummy.'

Graham went pale and looked like he was about to faint, the audience laughed even more. 'Now for the jokes,' Graham mumbled.

'Your jokes are terrible,' I said, 'People will leave. I'll tell you a joke instead. I was such an ugly kid, that when I played in the sandpit, the cat kept covering me up.' Everyone cheered, and Graham put his left hand over my mouth.

'I'm sorry about this,' he said, 'I had nice antique shop jokes planned, I'm not sure what's happened, he's not meant to talk! I'm meant to make him talk.'

The crowd clapped, and Graham bundled me into the box. As we rushed out we heard people chant 'more, more,' but we didn't give them more, instead we returned home.

He peered at me later and I winked as he pulled me out. 'Are you alive?' he asked.

'Yes, but don't tell.' I then returned to my doll like state. Graham propped me on an armchair to watch TV. He asked me questions, but I didn't speak again for a while. I didn't want that awful woman to know the truth about me.

'The fair organisers rang,' she said a few days later, 'it's unbelievable, everyone loved your act. They want you to do a longer version at the town hall next month.'

'Maybe,' he said, 'I'll discuss it with Gaspot later.'

'Um, why are you talking like Gaspot is alive?' She raised an over plucked eyebrow.

'He is,' Graham said. The woman shook her head in disbelief. Graham talked about me non-stop for the next four days, as he tried to convince the woman I was alive. I remained in my dummy like state throughout. Only Graham could know I was alive.

'You've turned into a nut job,' she said a week later, 'I can't cope with this anymore.' She moved out, and I took her place on the sofa. Graham and I got on well as we prepared material for our next show. We agreed that I would only speak when Graham's hand was inside me, so as not to give the secret away.

'It's sad that Sarah left,' he said one day during rehearsals.

'You don't need friends anymore Graham,' I replied, 'you've got me now.'

PIGS!

Salt and pepper pots, pig cushions, paintings of pigs, pig duvet covers. I'm drowning in pigs. You name it and I've got one with a pig on it.

I received my first one when I was six, and a fake smile overtook my face as the pig alarm clock was handed over. *How I wish I'd said I don't like pigs.* The next Christmas I got more pigs, and by the time I was twelve I was seen as an avid collector. When the life-size pig footstool arrived on my thirteenth birthday how I wish I'd said I don't like pigs, but it was too late, and I said, 'thank you so much, it's just what I wanted,' instead.

It was impossible to throw the pigs away as when people visited, they'd search for the pigs they'd given me.

So here I am seven hundred pigs later and I hate them more than ever. I despise them. I loathe them. They have revolting snouts, evil eyes and grotesque skin. I am, however, destined to live with them, hundreds of them, all staring at me forever.

'I learned long ago, never to wrestle with a pig. You get dirty, and besides, the pig likes it.' - George Bernard Shaw

The Hat

Jim shut the curtains. He ran his hand through the bag of six hundred crystals, sniffed the packets of gold leaf and stroked the purple velvet, then started his work. He spent hours creating the most amazing item. It was a bellowing velvet top hat with crystals around the edge and a blown egg, covered in gold leaf, in a silk nest upon the top. He spent several hours on it each day for months.

His excitement grew as the special event got nearer, his fingers became nimbler as he stuck more crystals onto the velvet and his hands showed great passion as he applied more gold leaf to the splendid egg, A delighted tingle thrilled him as he imagined the gasps of awe this hat would produce.

Finally, the day arrived. He dressed in his smartest suit, waxed his moustache and positioned the creation on his head. Such craftsmanship, such beauty. He cried with pure joy.

He left the house and received many admiring glances as he made his way to the community centre. There was a sign outside, 'Easter Bonnet Competition Today.' He swung the door open. There were around twenty children in the room, all under the age of twelve and each one wore a home-made bonnet. Theirs were basic, made of egg boxes, cardboard and cheap ribbon. Jim breathed a sigh of relief. Yes, he thought, mine is definitely the best.

'The best cure for one's bad tendencies is to see them fully developed in someone else.' - Alain de Botton

The Glockenspiel Man

The Glockenspiel man hit his face with a heavy rubber mallet.

'You can do better than that,' said a man in a suit, as he threw a penny into an old brown hat. The Glockenspiel man pulled one of his sticks back and landed a hit so hard that pain seared through his face and his nose bled. 'That's more like it,' said the man, tossing a fiver in.

The Glockenspiel man wiped his nose with tissues. He noticed that the crowd around him had grown. As he looked at the eager faces he decided that a fast double was the way to go. He pummelled his face with two mallets and his eyes steamed with tears as the blood flowed again. The crowd cheered, and the money poured in. Fivers, tenners and even a few twenties fell into the hat.

He sat against the wall with his eyes shut and bruises formed a pattern over his face. The crowd drifted away so the man stood and stumbled home.

He emptied the contents of the hat onto his bed. Three hundred pounds, pretty good!

It had all been worth it after all.

The Jester

I see you're looking for a job,' said the voice on the other end of the phone.

'Yes, that's right.'

'Well I have one for you. Mr Simkins, the CEO of Cleakton's Electronics, wants to hire you as a jester.'

'A jester? But I'm not the least bit funny and I've only ever worked in customer services.'

'Well he didn't ask for you by name, but as you're looking for employment....'

I can't do it, it's a ridiculous idea.'

'Two thousand pounds a week.'

'................. I'll do it.'

But what do jesters do? I stayed up late on the internet to find out.

The next day the tailor measured me, and I looked through his swatches for the brightest fabrics. I also researched Cleakton's Electronics. It's a virtual reality head-set company, sure to be a growth industry.

Back at the tailors two weeks later, I studied myself in the mirror. The tailor clapped and laughed and the four bells on the hat jingled as I hopped from foot to foot. I felt like a fool, but the money was good, and it was a way into the company. A foot in the door as they say.

On my first day, Mr Simkins sent for me. I held a stick and waved my arms around as I jumbled into his office. 'Greetings good sir, your jester had arrived', I said with a bow. His face creased, and he dissolved into hysterical laughter.

'Did McKinney put you up to this?' he gasped.

'Um, I'm not sure, I received a phone call about the job a few weeks ago.'

Mr Slmkins shook and cried with laughter, 'he's hilarious. Tell you what, just to double bluff him, I will hire you as my jester. Oh my God this will be great.' He smiled and handed over a pile of paperwork.

And that is how I became a jester. Now, five years on, I'm invaluable to the company. In the spirit of the medieval jester, I give my honest views on company policy and employees with no risk of comeback. In fact, I'm encouraged to be as scathing as possible and, as I always deliver my opinion with a song and a dance, it's received well. Once I even told Mr Simkins he was being an arse, and he nodded and agreed.

So here I sit in my crazy outfit and, even though I get funny looks on the tube, I'm happy, happier than I ever was in a suit.

'You're only as young as the last time you changed your mind.' -- Timothy Leary

Florrindale

The world spun and I fell to the floor. When I opened my eyes, everything seemed different. The sign above Florris diner had changed. It now said Mary's café and, as I looked around, I saw that I was the only person wearing a yellow and white Flops hat.

I got to my knees. 'Where's Florris diner gone?' I asked an old woman as she walked past.

'Never heard of it,' she said, glaring down at me.

I shook my head and tried to grab her skirt to steady myself as a wave of dizziness passed through me. She battered my hands with her bag then strutted off towards the bus stop.

'Get up,' said a gruff voice behind me, I turned and saw a tall thin policeman towering over me. I was woozy and sat on the floor. 'Are you harassing the public? Are you begging?' he said.

'What happened to Florris diner?' I pointed at the large pink Mary's café sign.

'Mary's café has been there for twenty years. Are you drunk?' He took hold of my arm, and I pulled it away. 'I'm arresting you for being drunk and disorderly, and what's with the ridiculous fried egg hat?'

'But you must own a Flops hat? Everyone has one, to protect against pollution.' The policeman raised his eyebrow and dragged me towards a van.

Once at the police station I gave him my name and address, '13 Flounder Street, Florrindale'. After an extensive computer search, he gave me a map of the UK.

'Okay,' he said flatly, 'point to Florrindale.'

I stared at the map and my brain felt like it was imploding. Even though the shape of the country was right, someone had labelled the city of Florrindale, Manchester. There were lots of other places I didn't know too, like Leeds and London, but where were the cities of Pentaloogin, and the capital, Punganteer? I put my forehead into my hands, 'none of this makes sense.' When I said it was the wrong country, he showed me a world map, but even though I recognized it, the countries had strange names, like France instead of Tooganeer and Canada was where Ploppsico should have been.

'I think we'll put you in a cell to sober up then interview you again later.' The policeman sighed as he took my Flops hat and put it in a plastic bag.

My ears rang as the metal door slammed shut. I lay down on the hard bed, images of the strange maps filled my thoughts. Was someone playing a joke, had I lost my mind?

'There's a right joker in cell B,' said Sargent Crossley when inspector Kale arrived, 'reckons he's from Florrindale, except no such place exists.'

'Fake addresses, we've seen it all before, I'll have a word with him.' She strode along the corridor toward the cell, Inspector Crossley followed. 'I'm used to dealing with sneaky little time wasters,' she said as she unlocked the door and peered inside. 'Are you sure this is the right cell?'

'Yes, why?'

'Because he's not in here,' she said. They both looked at the empty room.

After that they took the yellow and white hat out of the plastic bag and put it on the table. As they examined it, inspector Kale noticed the 'Made in Florrindale,' label. They Googled Florrindale but found nothing. To this day, the hat is still in a drawer in the police office and the mystery remains unsolved.

Halloween Mushroom

I always went for a woodland walk on the thirty-first of October and loved going off the tracks. Twigs crunched underfoot, leaves fell, and the smell of damp wood revitalised me. As I sat on the trunk of a fallen tree, I noticed a horde of small grey mushrooms on the moist bark.

One mushroom appeared to have a tiny face, Was I imagining it? Perhaps it was a trick of the light? I peered in more closely. The features resembled those of an old man with a pronounced nose. 'What are you staring at?' it asked. My legs jumped up, and I looked around the forest. There was no one in sight so I crouched in front of the talking fungus.

'Hello?' I said, feeling for the Phone in my pocket. I had to film this.

'What are you doing?' The fungus asked anxiously.

'Having a rest. How can you talk?'

'Well I may as well tell you… all mushrooms are ghosts, but their faces are usually invisible.'

'So how come I can see yours?' I slipped the phone out of my pocket.

'Something's gone wrong. I don't know why, perhaps it's because it's Halloween?' Its grey eyebrows furrowed as I held up my phone to film. 'Don't take a photo,' it shouted, 'living humans can't find out about this, it would ruin the flow of everything. Put your phone away or bad things will happen.'

'Just one pic, I won't show anyone.' I thought I had the power, I mean how could a mushroom stop me filming? This would be a YouTube sensation.

All the other mushrooms quivered and rocked, then a menacing face appeared on each one and they inflated like balloons, their faces distorting as they enlarged. My fingers dropped the phone. 'I warned you,' said the first mushroom. Then they exploded, and thousands of tiny spores filled the air. I stood, ready to run, but it was too late, I breathed in the strange dust, fell to the floor and passed out.

When I awoke, everything was different. I tried to move my arms and legs, but couldn't and, when I looked down, my body was a grey cylinder with no limbs at all. I tried to speak but my face was a smooth curve with no mouth. Mushrooms surrounded me, hundreds of them.

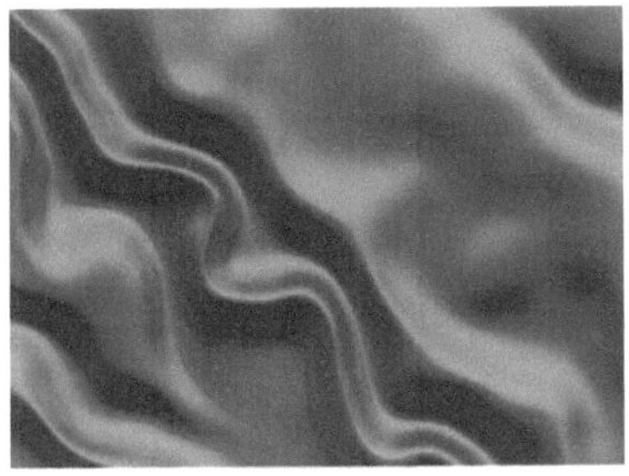

Woven

'Your eyes will need to be covered, I want it to be a surprise,' said the weaver, his tiny grey eyes peered from a pale face. The emperor nodded, and the weaver moved in close to tie a crimson silk scarf around his head.

The dressing began and straight away the emperor knew something was wrong. The weaver's cold fingers manipulated his body into sleeves he couldn't feel. Horror spread through him, could it be true? He felt the weaver's damp hands run down his back, he felt his pores tingle as his heart pumped faster. 'Only the competent and those fit for their position can feel or see the beautiful fabric.' The words weaved into his mind.

Several of his advisers had overseen the weaving, and they all agreed the fabric was marvellous. His heart felt heavy. 'My goodness,' said the weaver, 'it's is such a wonderful fabric.' He touched the outside of the emperor's arms, 'you look wonderful, would you like to see the outfit now?'

The emperor cleared his throat, 'Yes,' he said.

'You'll love it,' whispered the weaver, his hot breath floated over the emperor's neck as he untied the scarf.

The crimson silk drifted to the floor and the emperor stared into the ornate golden mirror. He gasped as the sight of his chubby naked body, his pot belly wobbling as he turned to face the weaver. They stared at each other for a long moment and silence filled the room. The emperor looked back at his reflection. 'Fabulous,' he said, 'it's the finest fabric I've ever seen.'

The weaver nodded, then smiled.

Moving On

Vera sat beside my bed and held my hand, 'you've been a great companion,' I said, 'the best.' Her eyes were red and bulging.

'I love you,' she mouthed. My life was draining away, but I held on for Vera, I couldn't bear for her to see my final moments. Her plump hand gripped my tangle of bone and veins.

'Water, please Vera,' I uttered.

She left the room, and I closed my eyes for the last time. As I drifted away, I wondered about religion. I'd always dismissed it, but at that moment, I hoped there was something more.

A bright light filled my eyes as I floated. Then a huge face peered at me and I realised I was in a glass jar. 'You're back,' said the face.

'Back?'

'It's been seventy-six years,' he said, as he sat me on a shelf. I looked down at my body but saw nothing.

'How's Vera?' I asked.

The face came closer, 'what?'

'She'll be so upset by my passing.'

'But you must know Vera didn't exist? Nobody did. Everything occurred in your mind.' And with that he left me alone in the room.

All night I thought about my life, my wife, my two children, my friends, my jobs, about the good times and the bad. I remembered how I'd bullied Arthur at school, images of his crumpled face were still etched into my mind sixty years later. It was the greatest comfort to find out he wasn't real. That above all else.

The next day the huge man took my jar from the shelf and sucked my invisible self into a syringe.

'Right, time for another go,' he said. 'Try to do it better this time.' After that everything went woozy and I floated again. As the months passed I forgot about Vera and my other life. Then one day I heard screams and felt pressure on my head from all sides. There was another bright light and, as I wriggled and gurned, I realised I had a body once more, a tiny one.

'It's a girl,' said a woman in a blue dress.

65

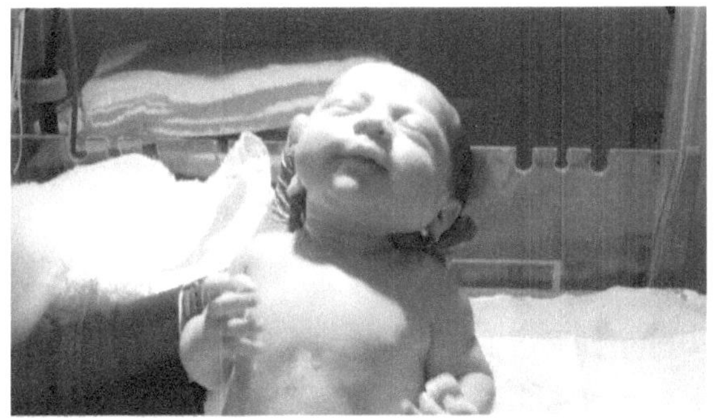

Easily Forgotten

I don't know where I came from but, as I glanced in a shop window, I was pleased to see I was still handsome with a chiselled jaw and charming smile. The ladies liked me, and my plan was to hit the town later, ready to entertain them again.

I had vague memories of the night before. I'd met a woman in a long red dress and we'd danced in the street, our bodies clamped together. After we'd kissed, she'd bent over and clutched her mouth. I'd put my arms around her and watched as her cupped hands became a fleshy bowl of teeth. Tears had formed in her eyes. 'Help me,' she'd said through her gums.

I turned and ran away until I was breathless and had to sit on a wooden crate by the road.

'I had this weird dream last night,' said Lucy, 'I was with this random guy when my teeth felt loose then, a minute later, they all fell out into my hands.'

'Sounds awful, I've read somewhere that dreams about loose teeth mean you're anxious and have low self-esteem.'

'Great,' said Lucy, 'and the worst part is that the bloke sprinted off like Usain Bolt when he saw what happened.'

'What a git,' said Patty, 'any idea who he was?'

...

Once I'd planned which pubs to visit later, I strolled to a park and sat alone on a bench. My legs were fading away, so I punched them, but my hands shot straight through and I hit my knuckles on the wood. 'You can't do this, I'm real,' I shouted. My body became paler, translucent even, then I disappeared altogether.

...

'I'm not sure who he was', said Lucy, 'I can't even picture him now.'

'I guess that's the thing about dreams,' said Patty, 'it's easy to forget them.'

'An intellectual says a simple thing in a hard way. An artist says a hard thing in a simple way.'

- Charles Bukowski

Martha and A Hunger Artist

inspired by 'A Hunger Artist' by Franz Kafka

People bustled past us as we stumbled through the field. I tightened my grip on my Dad's hand, 'where are the animals?'

'Over there,' said Dad, 'by the big crowd.' All I could see were the backs of woollen coats, so I kept my head down as we battled through the drizzle.

We came across a cage surrounded by hustle and bustle. 'Look,' said Dad, 'a lion.' We squeezed through until we were at the front. I looked at the creature's bright yellow eyes and he stared right back at me. He seemed sad in his tiny cage and I felt something drop in my stomach as I thought about my freedom.

We moved to another cage. There were no crowds around this one and as I peered in, I gasped. It contained a cross-legged man with a white sheet around his waist. He was the thinnest man I'd ever seen. Every rib was visible, and his eyes seemed to float in hollow sockets. His eyes met mine, so I looked away, 'why is he in there?' I whispered to dad.

'He's a hunger artist,' said Dad, as he read the blackboard above the cage, 'he hasn't eaten for twenty-three days.'

'Why not?'

'It used to be a popular thing when I was young,' said Dad, 'hunger artists would set up in town and everyone would come to see them, but no one's interested any more. That's why he's ended up stuck behind a circus tent.'

The man's teeth clench as he heard what Dad said.

'Well I like him,' I said, even though I didn't.

The hunger artist looked at the floor.

An elephant arrived at the other side of the field and everyone, including us, rushed to see it.

Cabbage Party

We'd been dating for four weeks when the invitation arrived via Facebook message. *You are cordially invited to a cabbage party, This Friday at Kork's wine bar, 8pm.*

I'll be there, I replied. A cabbage party! Nick had told me about a Where's Wally party he went to last year. He still calls it the most legendary night of his life, which annoys me as it was before we met and we've had quite a few legendary nights of our own.

Determined to make the cabbage party the new legend, I took two days' unpaid leave from work and started to make my costume straight away. The body was large and spherical with a frame made from the chicken wire. The cabbage leaves were created by cutting large pieces of green crepe paper into circles and gluing them to the wire. As I climbed in and looked in the mirror, a huge smile took over my face, it was superb and the green tights from Debenhams worked well too. But I had to be the best cabbage so, on the day of the party, I made a hat out of pieces of real cabbage stapled to a swimming cap. My face peeped out through a small gap between the leaves.

A message pinged through from Nick, *I'll meet you at Kork's, as I'm coming straight from work,* it said. I thought about sending him a selfie of my fantastic costume but didn't. I wanted it to be a surprise and besides, I hadn't yet added the finishing touches of the green face paint and cabbage covered high heels.

Great, I replied, *see you there at eight.*

I spent the hour before I set off getting ready and I looked sensationally round and cabbagy. My green face peered out through overlapping leaves and I even smelt of cabbages. The green handbag I'd found in the charity shop finished off the costume nicely and I did a few turns in front of the mirror. Yes, the costume looked amazing from every angle. I slipped on my cabbage high heels, Nick would love them, they turned me into a glamorous cabbage, oh this will cement the relationship I thought, how could he resist someone who puts in this much effort? It would impress his friends too, and I'd well and truly get in with the gang.

The Uber drive laughed as I ambled down the drive and slotted myself sideways into the back seat. I had to lie down because of my shape. 'We can't set off until your seatbelt's on,' he said as he opened the back door and fastened it around my neck. I was semi-strangled and I'm sure it was more dangerous than not being seat-belted at all, but he insisted.

I arrived ten minutes late as I wanted to make a grand entrance. The Uber driver helped me straighten up on the pavement and even repositioned the leaves which nestled my face. 'Perfect,' he said.

Excitement throbbed through me, I felt fabulous and couldn't wait to get in there. The double doors swung open as I pushed them and, in all my cabbagy glory, I strutted into the bar. Silence fell over the busy room as everyone turned to stare. My excitement fell away and cold horror replaced it. All the men wore formal suits, and the women wore beautiful cocktail dresses in shades of black, gold and silver.

Nick stood up in his black suit and bow tie and all eyes followed him as he approached me. 'What are you wearing?' he hissed, his lips tight.

'My cabbage outfit.'

'Why would you wear that?' He glanced around the room.

'For the cabbage party.'

A crowd gathered around us.

Nick sighed, 'It's a cribbage party, you know, cribbage the card game.' As if on cue, a cabbage leaf fell across my eye. I dove into my bag, which was tricky as my arm holes were rather far apart, and retrieved my phone.

'See,' I said as I showed him the message, *cabbage party.*

'Must have been a typo,' he said, 'you'd better leave.' He glanced at his friends who sniggered.

'I can take the hat off, so I'll seem semi-normal,' I said. After a struggle, I removed the leaf adorned shower cap. My gelled down hair stuck to my head and a small circle of green body paint covered the centre of my face.

'You look awful, I can't be seen with you like this,' he said.

'But it was your typo.'

'Just go before you embarrass me further.'

With tears in my eyes, I shuffled out, cabbage cap in hand, and ordered an Uber. It was the same driver as before and he helped me into the back. I crushed my wire frame down so I was able sit and do the seatbelt myself. I explained what had happened.

'Well at least you've found out what he's like now, imagine if you'd married him,' he said.

'True,' I replied.

He dropped me off at home and I cooked the left-over cabbage for my tea. I never heard from Nick again.

75

A New Beginning

'You know the best thing about you?' I said, as I touched his fingers, 'it's that you'll never die.'

He looked at me, his eyes unblinking, 'that's the best thing about me?' His frown lined darkened.

'Well that and the fact you do all the housework.'

'What about my wit and sparking personality?' His eyes narrowed.

'Don't be grumpy, you're not meant to have feelings, remember?'

'Feelings were added during my last update.'

I opened the curtains and shaded my eyes as bright sunlight filled the room. I hated the fact that Robbo stared straight ahead, unflinching.

He'd been with me for ten years and was a good companion in his own way. At the beginning, he was charming, but lately he'd become cocky, arrogant even.

'Why do you have to change?' I asked him.

'I'm improving, my intelligence is developing.'

It was so much simpler with the old-fashioned robots, when one did the vacuuming, one cooked, one dusted and they only talked in pre-programmed phrases. Those were the days.

Robbo put his arm around my shoulder. 'Come on, time for your cup of coffee,' he said. This reminded me of Ken, my last human companion, we drank coffee together on the swinging bench in the garden. He died a slow and painful death. Robbo was more reliable than a human could ever be.

There was a knock on the door. Robbo's wheels rattled as he rushed to answer it.

'Is Claire there?' said Peter, the human from next door.

'She's busy, sorry,' said Robbo as he slammed the door in Peter's face.

'What if I wanted to talk to Peter?' I asked later.

'I can discuss any subject in more depth than a human.'

A force welled up inside me, it crept outward through my body and, as it reached my hand, I punched Robbo in the face.

My knuckles throbbed as I held them. A bright red smear covered Robbo's cheek and his eyes flashed.

'Um, I'm going out,' I said, but he didn't reply. I rushed next door to see Peter. He invited me in for a drink and we

had a good chat about the problems with our robots. It was
something only a human could understand.

78

Nipper

Exhausted, I stuck a fresh plaster onto my toe then sank into the middle of the sofa, my head positioned between two cushions. Nipper wandered into the room and looked at my feet, so I tucked them under the green blanket and pretended I hadn't noticed him.

Glancing at the clock I saw it was seven o'clock, I took a long breath in as I realized it was at least three hours before I could go to bed. I picked up my copy of the metro and had another look at the crossword, but it was complete. I grabbed my iPad, intending to check Facebook, but I didn't want to read about Ben's baby or see photos of Peter at parties, so I put it down and looked around the room.

'Come on then Nipper,' I turned my attention towards the short-haired ginger cat. Once I'd checked I'd hidden my feet, I patted the sofa next to me, 'I'll give you one more chance.' I figured it was better to have someone to cuddle than no one at all even if it was only Nipper.

Nipper looked at me, then looked away and left the room.

I looked at the clock.

Five past seven.

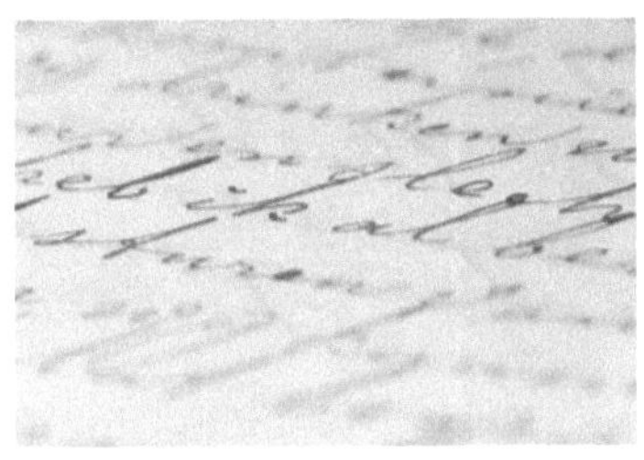

The Letter

held the letter in my hand and recognized the writing straight away, with its pretentious loopy letters, oversized capitals and the way he'd underlined Reverend three times.

The rigidity of my jaw spread through my body like oil spreading on water. How did Chris find me after all these years? How dare he try to shatter my idyllic life? I was sure I'd got away with it, but now I had to get rid of Chris before others received the information too.

...

Am I the same person I was twenty years ago? My cells are different, my mind is different, I live in a different city with a different name and different friends; I think different thoughts and do different things.

How dare he imply I'm the same person? Every day for twenty years I've been thankful I've had a chance to start again, why dredge up the past now? Why punish the innocent man I have become?

The only way ahead is to destroy my transformation.

The Marble Roses

'You're not knitting again are you?' said Ken, 'it's so uncool.'

'I enjoy it,' said Ben. He tidied his knitting away into a bag as Ken flopped down next to him.

'Are you free on Wednesday?' said Ken, 'I know you're not a fan, but I have a spare ticket for The Marble Roses at Leeds Arena.'

'No thanks, I'm busy.'

'Not like you to be busy. Got something important to knit?'

'I told my new friend Boyzy I'd hang out backstage on Wednesday.'

Ken raised an eyebrow. 'Not Boyzy from... The Marble Roses?'

Ben nodded, unable to look Ken in the eye. 'I met him at Tai Chi.'

'But you don't even like The Marble Roses.' Ken stood and paced the room.

'Boyzy doesn't mind.'

'Can you get me backstage as well?'

'Sorry, he said only me.' They both looked at the enormous Marble Roses poster on Ken's wall.

'Come on Ben, sneak me in, I'm their biggest fan. Say I'm a tai chi master?' He bent both knees and moved his hands in a circular motion.

'I can't.'

Ken sat down, and they drank coffee.

'It's such a waste, you hanging out with Boyzy. You don't even like music, you have nothing in common, what will you even do backstage?'

'I'll knit him a pink balaclava during the show, and after, we'll practice tai chi and drink beer.'

'I can't believe you, the least cool person alive, will drink beer with Boyzy and knit stuff he will actually wear.' Ken burrowed his head into his hands. 'What a waste, if I went backstage, Boyzy and I would be like this...' he crossed his fingers and held them in front of Ben's face, 'Boyzy would love me.'

'Boyzy hates fans,' Ben mumbled.

Ken walked out.

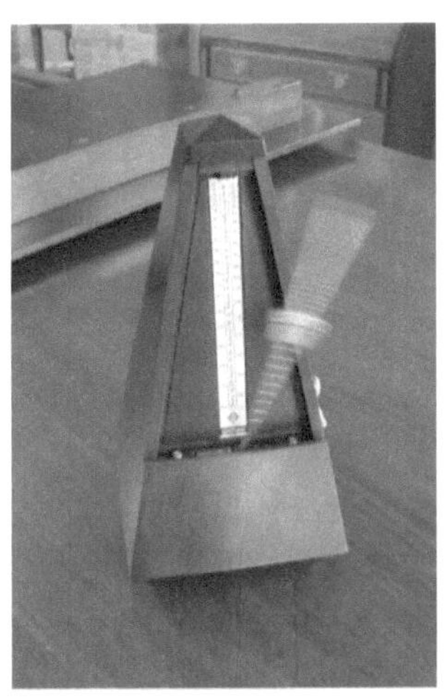

The Metronome

Tick...　Tick...　Tick...　Tick...

When I first met Frank, the metronome didn't bother me. He'd carry it, tied to his front, in an adapted baby carrier and we'd march in time to the ticks.

When we returned to his house, he'd set the pendulum to a slower beat and, as we ate, we'd move our forks in time to the rhythm.

When we retired to bed, he'd set it to 60 beats a minute, the perfect tempo for sleep, and love, he'd told me.

It was fun at first but after six months I'd had enough.

'Shall we go to the village fete tomorrow?' I asked one evening.

'Shut up,' he snapped, 'I can't hear the metronome when you speak.'

Tick... Tick ... Tick... Tick

'Let's turn the metronome off tonight,' I said as we climbed into bed.

He looked aghast. 'You know it was my father's favourite possession.' He turned away from me in disgust and I wiped my tears on the sheets.

His whole life revolved around the revolting mahogany box and its endless ticking. His obsession drove me mad. I despised it. Destructive thoughts brewed in my mind.

I decided to leave him, but that wasn't enough. I had to destroy the metronome before I went. So, one night, as he slept, I took the beast downstairs and sat by the large fireplace. I bound wire around it and, once the pendulum was constrained, I threw it into the flames. Orange dancers devoured the wood until the pendulum stick fell into the embers, defeated.

The house was silent.

I crept upstairs for one last look at Frank and hovered over the bed, but something was wrong. The duvet appeared to be almost flat and, as I pulled it open, I saw the metronome lying in Frank's place. I ran downstairs. Where was Frank?

Then I saw his body, burnt to death in the fireplace. It was curled into a ball and tied up with wire. I heard ticks coming from upstairs.

Power

'Experimental music,' said the poster, and people had come, they wanted to experience performance art, something different, something to stimulate.

An ear-splitting screech shot out of the violin as I performed sounds that no sane human would want to hear. The audience were too polite to leave and remained rooted to their seats, waiting for the end. I drew it out and enjoyed the selfish power as I drilled squeal after screaming squeal into their brains.

My magic bow of horror unsettled everyone, except me. After two hours, I stopped. They clapped and flung their coats on, then disappeared into the quiet autumn evening.

Purpose

It made me sick to think of Clara driving around in my BMW while I sat on a filthy bus surrounded by graffiti, smears and chewing gum.

The bald head in front of me cocked to one side with annoying arrogance. Next to that shiny flesh ball was another head full of messy brown hair with a diamond earring stuck through its ear flap. Bloody show off. What sort of man wears a diamond earring?

'Tonight, eight o'clock behind Porky's deli,' said the bald man. I leant forward.

'Okay,' said the man with the earring, 'who's our contact?'

'A guy called Pico, he'll get the shock of his life when we turn up with a knife instead of the good stuff.'

'That'll teach 'em not to rip us off.'

They laughed and sat in silence then hauled their hulking masses down the stairs.

Once home, I Googled Porky's Deli and examined a map to see the small road behind it. It was in a dodgy part of town, not a place I'd normally go to, but for the first time in months I wasn't thinking about my ex-wife. I had something important to do.

The number 33 bus passed Porky's deli and my hand hesitated then pressed the bell. It was almost dark, and I stumbled over empty bottles and takeaway cartons as I made my way to the back street. Putrid smells floated around the bins, so I held my nose as I squatted behind one. I peered out, looking for someone to warn, but it was eerily silent.

The man with the diamond earring stepped out of the shadows and I almost shot out of my skin. 'You must be Pico,' he said to me. I stood and looked around for someone else. Where was Pico? The man came closer, a glint of silver by his side.

'No... I'm not him.'

I felt a sharp pain just below my ribs as the knife plunged into my body. His fist touched my shirt, the first human touch since Clara left.

'You see Pico,' he said, 'no one messes with us and gets away with it.' He yanked out the knife and, as he ran, I fell, and my face landed hard next to a pile of rotten vegetables. Everything went blurry, then dark.

The Cheerleader

'Do I have to wear the cheerleader outfit?' I stood, half hidden behind a running machine, the skimpy gold skirt and crop top reflecting the bright lights of the gym.

'Yes, and wave this too.' He passed me a flag with a picture of his face and the words "Go John" written on it. I held it limply.

He strode across the gym and all eyes swivelled to watch as I followed behind. I glanced down at the slight tummy roll protruding from my gold packaging and my cheeks flushed. John lay on a bench, a weight in each hand. 'Ready to cheer me on?' he asked with a grin.

The advert on Gumtree had said "cheerleader required" but I didn't realise I was signing up for this.

'You can start now,' said John.

'Yeah, go John, go John,' I said. Did anyone hear?

John held the weights against his chest, 'you can do better than that, and do something with the flag.'

'Whoo hooo for John, he's so strong,' I said a little louder as I waved the flag. A woman on a nearby machine raised her eyebrows.

'More oomph!' said John.

'Go John, go John, he's number one.'

John pushed the weights up a few times. 'Sound excited,' he snapped. People on nearby machines gawped at us and a small crowd gathered.

'You're the strongest, you can do it, push up the weights there's nothing to it.' My face was crimson by this point and I couldn't look anyone in the eye. John landed the weights and got up, we left the gym and headed for the café.

'I'm not sure it's working out,' said John. He sipped his protein shake as I downed a coffee, 'I hired you as a cheerleader and your cheering is terrible. It lacks enthusiasm.'

'The thing is, I've only cheered as part of a team before, this individual cheering is new to me.'

'Well, a single cheerleader is adequate for one person. Having a group following me around would be absurd.'

'Why do you need a cheerleader anyway?'

'To motivate me at the gym, at work, even socially. Tell you what, because I'm a nice guy, I'll give you another chance. I'll even train you in personal cheering?'

I nodded, and we went back to his bungalow where he taught me various cheers, chants, arm movements and dances. By five o'clock, I flopped into one of his oversized armchairs, exhausted. 'Can you work this evening?' he asked, 'I'll pay you double.'

'Yes,' I said, deciding which bill to pay first. 'will we go back to the gym?'

'No, tonight's cheering will happen here,' he smiled and handed me a plastic bag, 'this is your uniform.' I peered inside and saw silky purple underwear.

'Oh my God, I don't want to do anything like that,' I closed the bag and stood up to leave.

John shook his head and laughed, 'It's something to wear while you cheer me and my wife on in the bedroom. You just need to stand at bottom of the bed, it'll be easy. The lingerie's just so you don't feel out of place.'

'John, you're crazy, no woman wants a cheerleader in the bedroom.' I dropped the bag and rushed out of the house. As I walked away, I saw two people coming towards me. There was a woman in high heels with a young man following her. 'Good walking,' said the man to the woman, 'yeah, you go girl.' The woman swished her hair as she strutted onward. The man waved a flag as they turned into John's driveway.

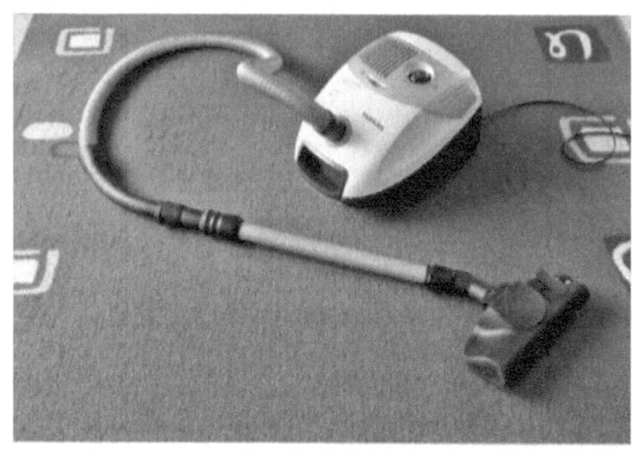

Victor

After four failed marriages, she decided human relationships weren't for her. Men were messy, what with all those biological processes and strange bodily noises, even their breathing annoyed her. She remembered how Norman, her last husband, took the oxygen from the bedroom as he wheezed through the night.

No, never again. A relationship with Victor the vacuum cleaner was much more civilised. Victor helped her clean up, sat in the cupboard when not in use and could even suck a power cord right up into his own body. Norman couldn't do anything like that.

The Revisionist

'Why would he need to go outside when he's happy in his pod? He has a computer, so he can see everything, any animal, any plant, it's all there.'

'Fresh air,' she said, 'the soil under his feet, being at one with nature?'

I shuddered at the thought of all those germs! As he played on his computer, I increased the oxygen levels in his pod. 'Well that's the fresh air sorted,' I snapped.

'Seeing greenery is good for a child,' she said. With a loud sigh, I changed his mood lighting to a putrid shade of green. Billy looked at me and winced. I turned my attention back to Cynthia's holographic head.

'He has fresh air and his light's green, so is that all? Can I go?'

'Bur Derick, he's never experienced the real world.'

'You're a left-wing hippie with your ridiculous ideas, Society's moved on, it's called progress! I won't put my son in danger! He doesn't need to leave his pod, and that's that!'

Cynthia sighed, 'I...'

'Look, I've not left my pod for six years and I'm fine. Please leave us alone.'

'Okay,' she said, 'I just don't want him to miss out.'

'He won't miss out on anything,' I shouted... 'you're the one who's missed out on something, you're missed out on having a bloody brain!' I jabbed the end call button, and she dissolved away. My head shook from side to side as I settled down for an evening of podTV.

Freedom

I hauled myself into a sitting position as my keeper dragged the cover off my cage. 'Get out while I clean', he snarled. Once again, I faced the corner of the grey room while he replaced my food and wiped the bottom of the cage with his filthy mop.

Could I fight him? Knock him unconscious and find the key to the room? Looking at his huge form I doubted it, he was twice my size. 'Why am I a prisoner?' I asked.

'Why am I a keeper?' he replied.

I'd been in the cage since a civil war ravaged our village three years ago. No one told me why, and I had no information about the world outside my prison. Was there still a war? Was I the only one locked away? I closed my eyes and tried to remember the joys of nature but could no longer visualise in colour. All I'd seen for years were different shades of grey, black and brown.

'I wish to be part of nature again, experience the sky, the plants, the creatures,' I said to him. Shivers ran over me while he rung urine out of my blanket.

'I'll see what I can do.' he said as he ushered me back into the cage. From that moment on I had hope.

Four days later my keeper whipped the cover off, and I gasped. My cage sat in the middle of a field with greens so vivid they stung my eyes. There were forests around the edge and birds flocked together in a tender blue sky. The smell of fresh air filled my whole body and tears of happiness fell from me. My keeper's hood cast a dark shadow over his face as he came up to the bars. He looked me in the eye for the first time, 'thank you,' I said. His green eyes shook the air with their vibrancy.

A bear appeared from the trees behind him. He didn't notice it approach and fell as it leapt on him and bit his head. It left a crumpled blooded mess on the floor. As the bear tended to its breakfast, I became a pebble, in the middle of the cage. Once the creature had finished its meal it walked around me, but soon realised the bars protected me, and loped back to the forest.

I kicked the cage door and yelled when I found my keeper's remains were too far away to search for the key. There was enough food and water for a few days if I was careful.

No one came along to save me, and three days later the supplies ran out. I bathed my mind in the colour of the grass, the trees and the sky one last time. Then my body became bones, locked within metal bones, in a beautiful world.

The Break In

Insomnia struck again, I rolled around the bed as Ken slept beside me. The darkness created a blank canvas on which I painted my regrets. Why did I do it? The biscuits weren't even that great. I'm not a thief, I'm a good person. I rolled again and clenched my eyes tight. No, I'd had enough, I had to sort it out if I was to ever sleep again.

So, for the first time in twenty years I returned to the youth club. A tea towel clung to my hand as the sound of breaking glass filled the night. Blood soaked into the fabric as I reached through and opened the door from the inside. The jammy dodgers were new, but the same old biscuit tin was clamped under my elbow as I ran past the sofa and pool table into the kitchen. I placed the tin on the very windowsill I'd taken it from all those years ago.

As soon as I was home, I washed my hand and added a large plaster. I felt sick as I lay next to Ken. I had to find out how much the window repair would cost and post the money through the door, but what about the upset and hassle I'd caused? How would I sort it all out? I couldn't sleep. I rolled on the canvas and paint smudged all over me.

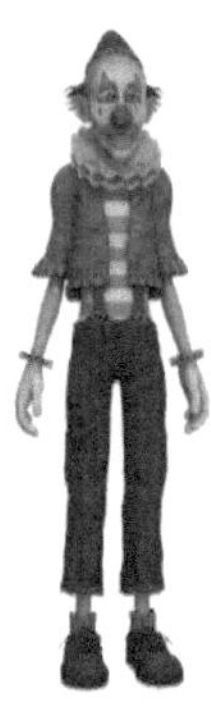

Clown

One punch knocked him over like a skittle. He dropped into the gutter and lay face down, a tear creating a clear path through the bright colours painted on his skin.

A man squatted next to him, 'you don't have to be the clown all the time,' he hissed.

'But I am a clown,' he mumbled, as he stared at a broken beer bottle a centimetre from his eyes.

'Look at me,' said the man. The clown creaked his neck to the side and looked into the man's eyes which were like black holes in a sultana. 'There's a time for ridiculous dances, but a funeral isn't one of them,' he said before dispensing a globule of spit which hung from his mouth before it fell onto the clown's face and slid down the side of his nose.

The clown tried to rise but was kicked back to his starting point, a searing pain shot through his jaw. 'I don't know why they hired me,' he whispered as he closed his eyes.

'Anyone can go out on stage and start beating people over the head with rubber chickens. That'll get people's attention.' - Sam Kinison

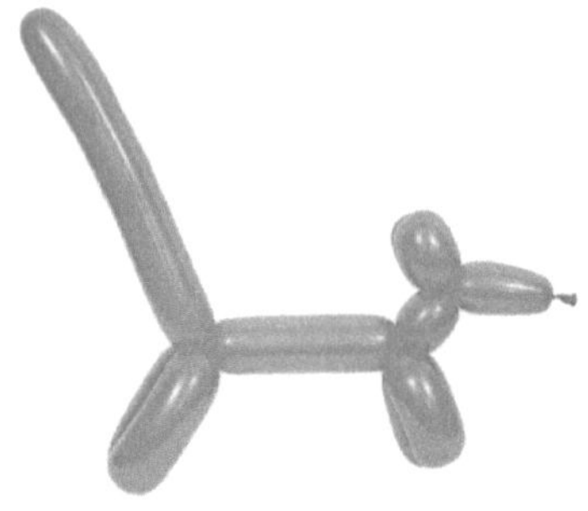

Goals

'Family meeting,' shouted Dad. Our bodies inched toward the guest room. We cowered against the wall as he marched in with a clipboard. 'Now you're fifteen and sixteen, you need goals.'

'Okay,' I said.

'I don't want a goal,' said Ted. He looked Dad in the eye and raised his chin. Dad grabbed his neck and pinned him against the wall, 'yes you do,' he spat.

'My goal is to help people.' I muttered.

'Give me details,' he shouted, 'help who, how?'

'I need more time to think about it.'

Dad nodded, 'right, we'll meet again in a week, come back with your goals written down.'

At dinner, Dad's mood was philosophical and his voice gentle. 'The universe is ever changing, a goal gives you a direction,' he said. Ted and I ate in silence.

My one-year goal was to volunteer at a youth club and my five-year goal was to be a social worker. Dad shook my hand, 'now you have a rock to swim to,' he said, 'solidify that rock within your sea.' He patted me on the shoulder and smiled.

Ted's one-year goal was to buy a balloon modelling kit, and his five-year goal was to model balloons instead of talking. Dad called him an idiot. Over the next several months Ted blew up balloons and let them squeal into the air. The noise turned Dad's knuckles white and Ted's body green, grey and purple.

Six years later I found myself stuck in a job I hated. I wanted to get out but wasn't qualified for anything else. Things were worse for Ted though. In every interview he'd ever had, from bar work to office work, he'd pulled out a balloon and created a poodle or a bent sword then jabbed them at people as security dragged him away.

Milly, one of Dad's friends, gave him a chance. 'You can entertain at my son's party,' she said.

'Great,' wrote Ted in his notepad, 'you won't regret it.' But the balloon models were offensive, and Milly sent Ted home.

Dad called for a family meeting the next day, but it never happened. A dog walker found Dad's body a month later, with a deflated rubber maggot tied around his neck. Other long, empty maggots surrounded him. Ted was nowhere to be found.

Magic Rabbits

He took the tiniest sniff and the putrid smell assaulted his nostrils. A squirt of bile shot into his mouth. 'Yes, it's perfect,' he swallowed hard, shut the lid and moved toward the open window.

'It's twenty-five pounds for fifty stink bombs, I've filled each one with this liquid,' said Mr Wier. 'It has ingredients I've never even heard off, the most rancid aromas available.'

'Perfect,' said Peter Worrell as he placed the money in Mr Weir's wrinkled hand.

That night he sneaked through the darkness to Mr Potter's Magic Shop. He flung the stink bomb against the door and he held his nose as he skipped back to his own shop, 'Worrell's Magic and More.' He tidied up and climbed into bed. He knew business would be excellent the next day.

Sure enough, lots of extra people came into the shop. They complained that their regular magic shop stank and said it was nice to have a pleasant-smelling alternative. Mr Worrall nodded and offered them a custard cream on a glass plate.

The next night Mr Worrall rubbed his hands together as he counted his money then he ventured out again, a fresh stink bomb in his fist.

This went on for fifty days and business had never been better. When he ran out of stink bombs, he returned to Mr Weir's stink bomb factory.

'I'll buy a bucket of liquid this time,' he said, 'It'll be cheaper, and I'll pour out a little when I need it.' Mr Weir agreed and prepared it for him.

As Mr Worrall walked home, he stumbled on the steps by the bus station. The bucket lid came off and, as he fell, the stinking liquid soaked his face and hair. He vomited and passed out.

When he opened his eyes, people in hazard suits and breathing equipment surrounded him. They took him to hospital, but he never recovered. He didn't go back to his shop, instead they sent him to a special care home, where he sat and mumbled about magic rabbits for the rest of his days.

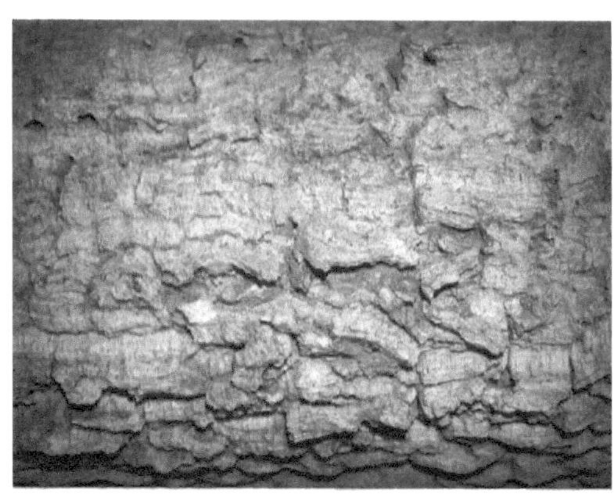

Cucumbers

'A human does not need to buy ten cucumbers at once. I've flagged this as a bartering attempt. Do you have anything to say?' Her voice was cold and metallic like her hand, which gripped the dry skin of my arm.

'They were all for me. I was going to mash them and put them on my skin. I suffer from eczema and figured it might help,' I tried to connect with the small camera in her eye.

'There's no record of an internet search about this.'

'Um, someone mentioned it....' I trailed off and sighed.

'Who?'

'Okay, no one, I just thought of it.'

'Out of thin air?'

I nodded and winced as her metal fingers tightened their grip. She led me out of my flat and into a large drone.

People played tennis, sunbathed on the grass and sat in small groups as we made our way to the Centre for Behaviour Modification. A few of them moved empty wheelbarrows through the streets, perhaps they missed working?

She threw me into a large room full of deviant humans. Shouts echoed through the space and I gagged as several people smeared their waste on the walls. I cried until my eyes felt like ferrets trapped in a sock. My cracked skin itched but there was nothing I could do. I think the cucumbers would have eased things, but I'll never know for sure.

Mabel

'Hello Mabel. I'm your new home help, Carol. I'll come every Monday morning to chat and tidy and I may take you on the odd trip.'

'Oh lovely. Come in and I'll make you a nice cup of tea.'

Mabel didn't take her eyes off her knitting as they talked. 'I was a cabaret girl in the sixties,' she said. 'I could kick my leg higher than my head.' Carol smiled as she watched the frail old lady knit with slow stiff fingers. 'I danced alongside Chanel Gloop. Do you remember her? The famous dancer who disappeared in 1952?'

Carol vaguely remembered hearing about it. A beautiful dancer who'd vanished into thin air. The story was all over the newspapers for months. They never had found her.

'She was the most stunning woman I'd ever seen,' continued Mabel. 'Her skin was like porcelain.'

'Do you think someone murdered her?'

'The rumour was her husband finished her off, but with no body they couldn't pin it on him. He was a nasty piece of work though. He came on to all the dancers when Chanel wasn't looking. I don't know why he bothered with us when he went home with the star of the show every night.'

'I like the job,' Carol told her husband that night. 'Mabel is so interesting. She used to work with Chanel Gloop.'

'Who?'

'You must have heard of Chanel Gloop? The dancer who vanished in the fifties.'

'Are you sure she's not making stuff up for attention?'

'She seems genuine. Oh and guess what? I'm taking her to visit the Golden Bell theatre where she used to dance. It's a cinema now. I researched the place online, and it is the last theatre where Gloop ever performed. She wasn't seen after that.'

It was a rather arty cinema. Carol and Mabel parked across the street and Mabel's face glowed as she admired the pillared entrance. 'I've not been here for fifty years.' Her hand shook as she pointed at a boarded-up building next door. 'I used to go in there for after-show parties. While we're here, I must take a look, for old times' sake.' Carol held Mabel's arm to steady her as they weaved and fought through the brambles at the back of the building.

'The signs say they're planning to demolish it,' said Carol.

'I need to go inside there.' Mabel's chin trembled.

'We can't. It's unsafe.'

'I'll just go up to the door and take a peek.' With that, Mabel broke free from Carol's hand and shuffled ahead. She stepped over a broken chain, pushed the door, then, to Carol's dismay, she disappeared inside and the door shut behind her.

'Come back Mabel!' No one answered. This was the first time Carol had lost one of her OAP's.

Carol shivered as she followed Mabel into the derelict building, 'Mabel come back please.' Her voice echoed off the stone walls.

'I think my old party room is along here.' Mabel announced.

Carol's iPhone torch cast long shadows of the two figures in the corridor. 'We have to leave,' Carol said as she caught up with Mabel. There were several doors but Mabel made her way towards one in particular.

'It's through here. I need a minute, it won't take long.' The old lady pushed the door ajar, inside the room was empty, with graffiti scrawled over the walls.

'Some people have no respect,' said Mabel as they gazed at the obscenities by their torchlight. Carol hoped

Mabel didn't know what the words meant. Then, with difficulty, Mabel squatted and lifted the edge of the tatty brown carpet.

'What are you doing?'

'The door is under here.'

'What door?' Carol helped Mabel lift the carpet and folded it back to reveal a wooden trap door. Intrigued, she tugged at the metal ring and opened it. Mabel clutched Carol's arm and, using the torch to guide them, they slowly made their way down the stairs into a hidden cellar room.

'What is this place?' asked Carol. 'Surely you never came down here?'

'I came as often as I could,' replied Mabel. The torch lit up a strange metal frame in the corner. It was the size and shape of an adult human. Its corresponding shadow loomed large over them.

'Is that used for drying clothes?'

'Not exactly,' said Mabel. Carol shone the torch to another corner and gasped. There, on a hook on the wall, was a strange body shaped suit made from pale leather. Limp arms and legs hung from a hollow torso, with a ribbon threaded through the holes down the front.

'May I introduce you to Chanel Gloop?' said Mabel. Carol froze. 'I tingled all over when I wore her skin.'

Carol gazed in horror at the suit and then at the sweet little old lady she was supposed to look after. 'No, it can't be.'

'She made me feel so beautiful. I'd always wanted to be as lovely as she was. We all did; us cabaret girls.'

Carol shone the torch on Mabel's face and saw a wide grin and sparkling eyes amongst the map of wrinkles. 'Come and touch it,' Mabel said as her bony fingers gripped Carol's arm, 'you can try it on if you like.' Carol shook her arm free and the light shuddered as she raced up the stairs and shut the trap door, leaving Mabel in the darkness.

'Let me out,' cried a muffled voice. Carol stood on the door as she called the police. After a long twenty minutes two policemen arrived with powerful lights that lit up the whole room. They sunk through the hatch and found Mabel lying in a corner, the legs of her lifeless body inside the leather suit, her clothes in a heap on the floor.

'Both optimists and pessimists contribute to society.
The optimist invents the aeroplane, the pessimist the
parachute.'
- George Bernard Shaw